To Mindy and Leslie —B.M.

To Joseph, Edie, Noah, and especially Sara —A.K.

Text copyright © 2000 by Barbara Maitland
Pictures copyright © 2000 by Andrew Kulman
Distributed in Canada by Douglas & McIntyre Ltd.
Color separations by Hong Kong Scanner Arts
Printed and bound in the United States of America by Worzalla
Typography by Rebecca A. Smith
First edition, 2000
1 3 5 7 9 10 8 6 4 2

Library of Congress Cataloging-in-Publication Data
Maitland, Barbara.
    Moo in the morning / Barbara Maitland ; pictures by Andrew Kulman. — 1st ed.
        p.   cm.
    Summary: Tired of all the loud city noises early in the morning, a mother and child
visit a farm, where very different noises greet them when the sun comes up.
    ISBN 0-374-35038-8
    [1. City and town life—Fiction.   2. Farm life—Fiction.   3. Animal sounds—Fiction.
4. Domestic animals—Fiction.]   I. Kulman, Andrew, ill.   II. Title.
PZ7.M27885Mo   2000
    [E]—dc21   97-17354

BARBARA MAITLAND
MOO IN THE MORNING

PICTURES BY ANDREW KULMAN

FARRAR STRAUS GIROUX　　NEW YORK

Here in the city,
the big, bright, busy city—

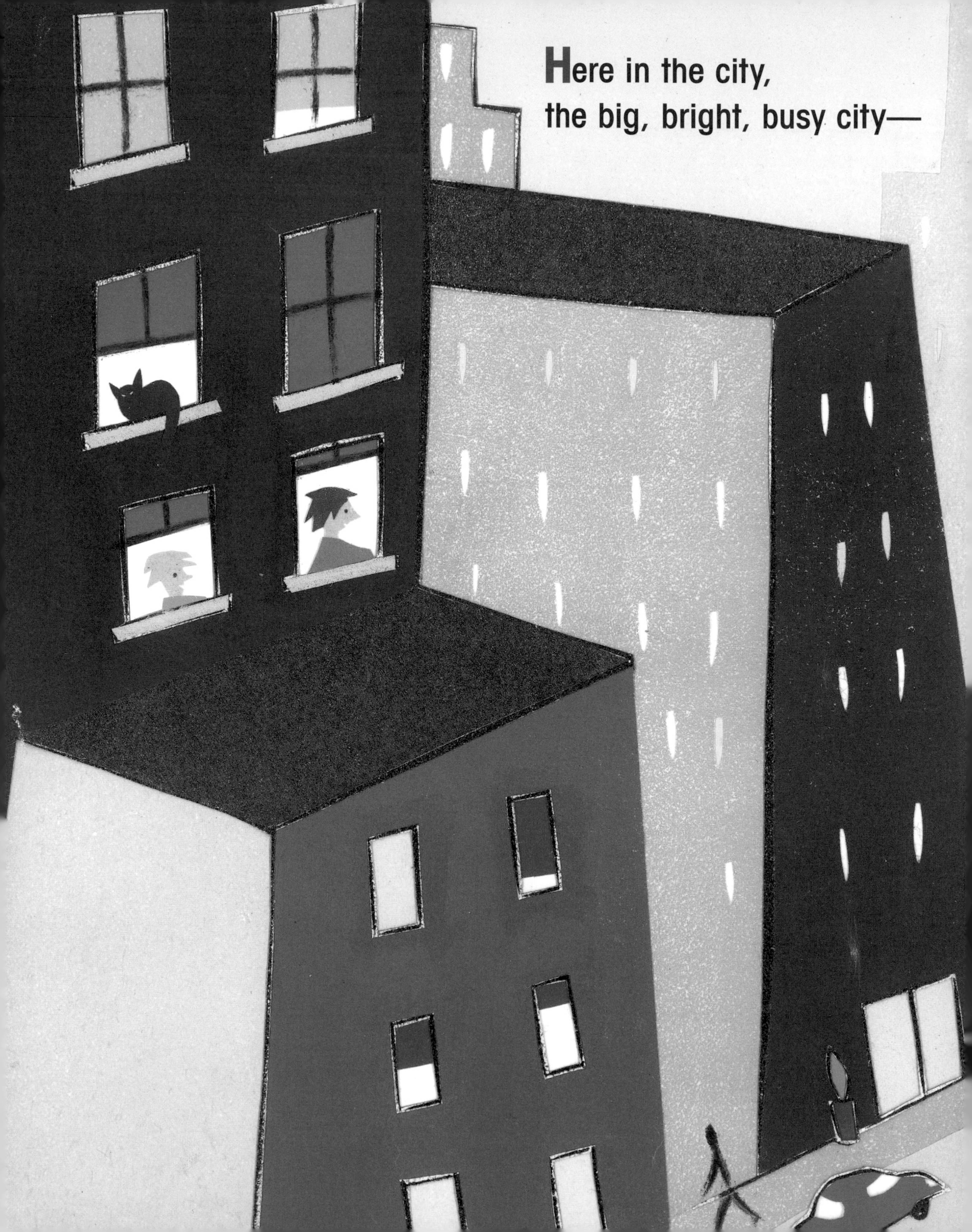

the big, bright, busy, NOISY city,

There are clangings and clashes,
and rattles and rumbles
early in the morning.

Mom says it's loud here.
She likes city noise,
but not first thing.
Not so early in the morning.

She says we'll visit
Uncle Jack at his quiet
farm in the country.

In the day, the farm is fun.
There's a pond to swim in and a barn to hide in,

fields to play in and trees to climb.

But it's quiet and dark
when we go to bed—
how will we know when it's morning?

"Ooom-moooo!"
And again!
"Ooom-moooo!"
What's that?

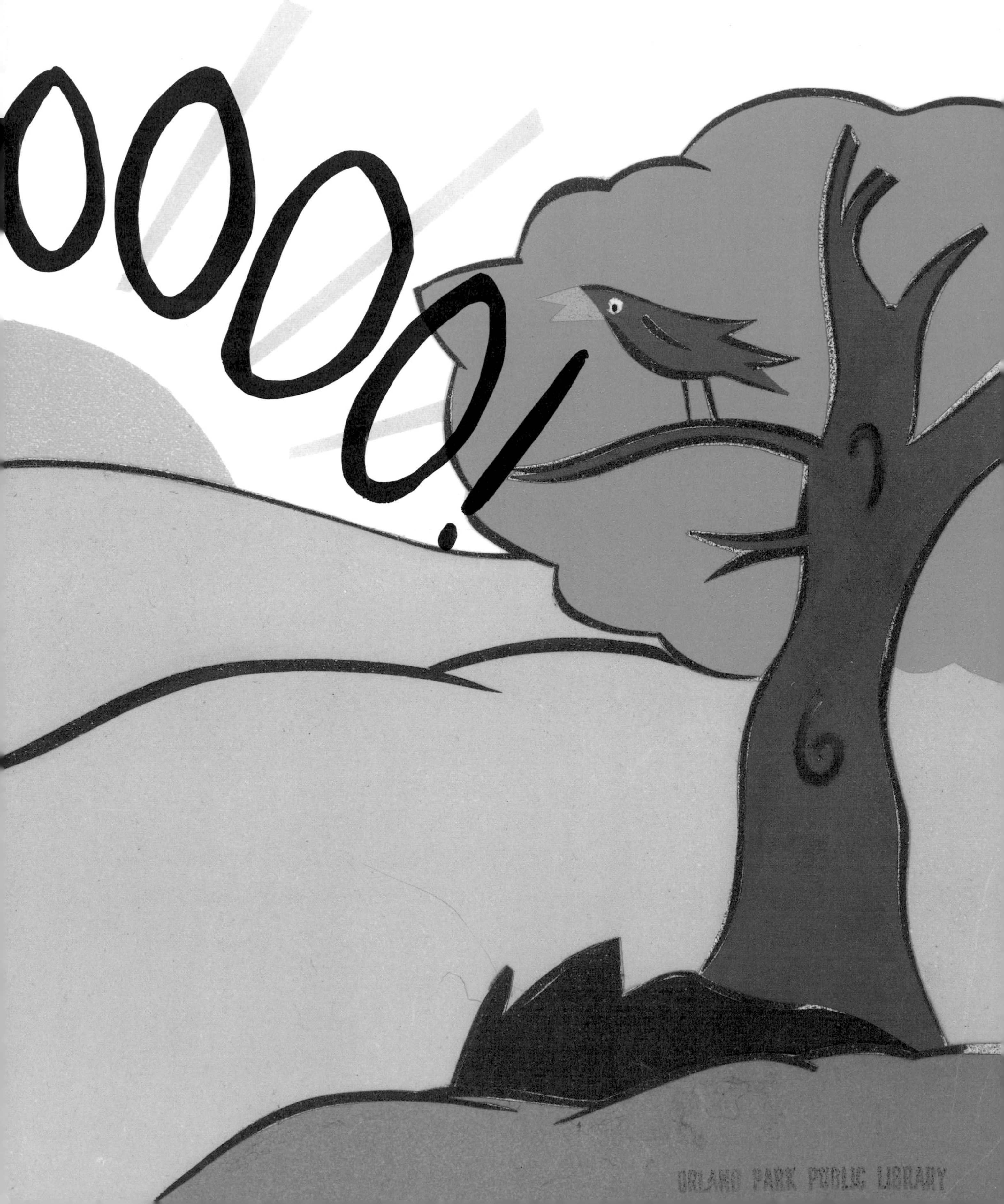
oooo!

It's a cow saying "MOOO!" in the morning!

Then the rooster crows,
"Cock-a-doodle-doo!"

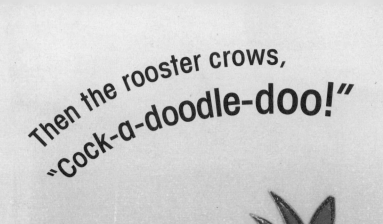

And all the cows
moo in the morning.

A sleepy "Tweet,"

and all the birds sing

with a twitter and a chatter,

with the "Cock-a-doodle-doo!"
and the "Ooom-moooo!"
early in the morning.

Next to wake are the ducks and hens—

"Quack!" with a splash! and "Cluck, cluck, cluck!"

Ducks all quacking,

hens all clucking,

birds all tweeting,

rooster crowing,

and those mooers mooing in the morning.

The sheep wake "Baa!"
And the lambs wake "Bleat!"

"Baa!"

"Bleat!"

"Quack!"

"Cluck!"

"Tweet! Tweet! Tweet!"

"Cock-a-doodle-doo!"

And you-know-who going
"Moo, moo, MOOO!" in the morning.

Now the tractor is rumbling
and pots and pans are banging
and doors are slamming

and it's tweety, and quacky,
and clucky, and MOOEY
early in the morning.

Mom says it's time to go.
She likes the farm, but not that mooing
early in the morning.

Home in the city.
The big, bright, busy city.

The big, bright, busy, quiet city.